Lady Rose

Written by:
Stephen Cosgrove
Illustrated by:
Robin James

A Serendipity™ Book

PRICE STERN SLOAN
Los Angeles

Dedicated to the memory of Cara Knott. Her message was floated to me on the petals of a bright red rose.

Stephen

It was in the sea that this story began. It was in the sea that this story did end.

In this sea called the Sargasso Sea sat an island called Serendipity. In its majesty the sea roared and rolled to the shores of this island, as if to gently touch the sands with the memory of all things past.

Surrounding all was the sea, beautiful crystalline water that seemingly wrapped the Island of Serendipity in a shawl of surging ivory-laced blue.

There were many creatures that lived in the sea off the shore of Serendipity. There were whales that breached high into the air only for the exhilaration. There were dolphin that darted about chasing silver-finned fish that flashed like lightning in stormy seas. There were seals that barked like dogs and laid on the rocks and jetties to soak up the warmth of the sun.

Most special of all were the otters that lived in meadows of kelp that floated at the surface and protected an abundance of good things to eat below. They frolicked in the froth and foam of the sea seemingly only to entertain you and me.

The odd thing about all of these creatures from the sea was that they seemed to be waiting—waiting for a message to come to the sea from the Island of Serendipity. They floated idly where the freshwater river slipped silkily into the sea, teased with scents of things none of them had seen before and could hardly imagine.

It was here that all of these creatures waited and wondered for some message from one who had gone before. They waited and wondered—whale, seal, dolphin and otter—waited for some sign from Lady Rose.

Years before, it seemed, there was a beautiful, sinewy otter that lived in the rich waters of the Sargasso Sea. Her fur was the color of sunshine gold and her eyes, unlike the other otters', were blue as the sky was blue. When she swam, she sliced through the water like a bird in the sky. She was silly like soda bubbles through and through, and her laughter could bring a smile to a clamshell, it was true. Loved by all was she and they called her Lady Rose.

Lady Rose loved all things that were beautiful and sought them out wherever they might be. The most beautiful thing to her was knowledge—knowing the who, why, what, when and where of anything and everything.

She was not content to sit idly by and wait for things to float to her on the tides. Lady Rose would boldly swim where others wouldn't dare to go. She would leap high into the air to see if she could see a reflection in the eye of a gull. She would dive deeper than deep down into the sea just to ask a question of a feather-finned eel.

For there was not a question without an answer to the curious Lady Rose.

One day as she swam near the mouth of the river, sniffing a bit of this and that, she thought of a question that had never been answered before, "Where does the water come from that flows into the sea?"

Like a beckoning beacon, the question drew her to the answer. As she started to swim up the river, away from the sea and all that she knew, a whale called to her, "You ought not go, little otter. Where you will find the answer, you will want to stay, and you never will come back this way."

"Oh, ho!" laughed Lady Rose. "Once the question is answered, I won't stay."

With a flip and a splash, she began the journey away from the sea and up the river. At first things stayed the same, and then slowly everything began to change. Where the sea was salty, these waters were fresh and pure. Where the sea was wrapped in the foam of storms passed, these waters were crystal clear.

All about were scents and smells the likes of which Lady Rose had never smelled before. But in the water there was still this burning question of where it all began.

The farther she went from the sea, the less there was of the sea in the water. These waters flowed rather than surged. These waters were quiet where the sea shouted with songs to be sung.

Here finger willows trailed their gentle limbs in the water. Here blossoms from the water lily scented air and water alike. But here was not the answer nor the end of the journey, and she pressed on farther up the river.

She hadn't been swimming long when she was stopped by a manatee who sang, "You ought not go, little otter. When you find your answer, you will want to stay, and you never will come back this way."

"Oh, ho!" laughed Lady Rose. "Once the question is answered, I won't stay." And she quickly swam away.

On and on she swam until she came to a place where the river split into several small crystal streams. Without thought or worry she followed a smaller stream, fresh now with more questions and the promise of answers to come. Farther and farther she swam, away from the sea.

She had moments of doubt and often murmured, "I otter go back, but I've just got to know the answer." Then, as always, she swam on.

The journey was not easy. Time and time again she slithered and slipped up and over waterfalls washed in bowers of flowers. Rock by rock she clambered and climbed as the water raced by gurgling loud warnings, "You had better go back! You had better go back!"

But Lady Rose paid little heed and continued her quest.

Finally, when she thought her journey would never end, Lady Rose came to the beginning where the stream didn't flow any more. It was here that the crystal waters bubbled up from the ground in a rock-lined pool. It was here that she found growing all around the pool…red, red roses. The smell, the scent, the perfume was heady and so sweet, so light, that Lady Rose nearly swooned in delight.

It was here that the river began. It was here that her journey ended.

There weren't just flowers here, there were animals of every sort created by nature. Here they frolicked; here they played. Lady Rose spun around the pool in dizzying circles as tears of joy welled in her eyes.

"Oh, ho," called a blue jay from the tree. "Why do you cry, little otter?"

"Because," laughed Lady Rose, "everyone told me 'You ought not go, little otter. When you find the answer, you will want to stay, and you never will come back this way.' And I told them I could go and that I wouldn't stay, but now that I have seen what I have seen, I don't want to leave. If I leave, I fear I will not find my way back here."

"Ah," said the bird, "then you must stay."

"But my friends will worry," lamented Lady Rose.

"Not if you send them a note, a message, letting them know that you arrived okay." And with that the bird fluttered away.

Lady Rose thought and thought of a way that she could send a message to her friends in the sea—a message letting them all know that she was okay. But what should the message say and how could it be delivered?

She tried telling butterflies the secret, but they were so fluttery there was no guarantee that they would deliver the message. She tried teaching the birds a new song, but they kept changing the words and, once again, the message couldn't be delivered.

She thought and she thought and finally she came up with the most marvelous plan, the most marvelous plan indeed.

Relieved that her friends wouldn't worry, Lady Rose frolicked in the waters that bubbled from here...the beginning and the end of the sea.

IN LATE SPRING OR EARLY SUMMER
LOOK FOR THE MESSAGE THAT SHE CHOSE
FOR FLOATING ON THE WATERS
ARE THE PETALS FROM LADY ROSE

Serendipity Books

Written by Stephen Cosgrove
Illustrated by Robin James

Enjoy all the delightful books in the Serendipity Series:

The above books, and many others, can be bought wherever books are sold, or may be ordered directly from the publisher.

PRICE STERN SLOAN
360 North La Cienega Boulevard, Los Angeles, California 90048